Leapfrog Rhyme Time

# Pets on Parade

by Jillian Powell

Illustrated by Gwyneth Williamson

W
FRANKLIN WATTS
LONDON•SYDNEY

Bring
your
Pet to
school

It was "Bring Your
Pet to School" day.
Most children brought a pet.

5

There were dogs and cats and rabbits,

# and a cheeky marmoset.

Sam had brought
his hamster.

It was running
round its wheel.

May had brought
her kitten.

It thought the hamster
was a meal!

Dan had eight
stick insects.

They looked
like lots of sticks.

But two got out along the way ...

# then there were only six!

Jenny had a tiny mouse.

She kept it in her pocket.

But when the mouse
saw all the cats,

it shot off like a rocket.

Toby had a ferret.

He had taught it
how to roll.

But when the ferret saw
the mouse ...

both vanished

down a hole!

Then in came Ricky Brown.

He was carrying a box.

What could be inside it?

A tortoise or a fox?

And everyone began to scream as Ricky let it out ...

the biggest snake
they'd ever seen was
slithering about!

Dogs were playing.
Cats were chasing.

28

They were making
such a noise.

Then Miss Brett stood up and shouted,

30

"Take your pets home,
girls and boys!"

Leapfrog Rhyme Time has been specially designed to fit the requirements of the Literacy Framework. It offers real books for beginner readers by top authors and illustrators.

## RHYME TIME

**Mr Spotty's Potty**
ISBN 978 0 7496 3831 3

**Eight Enormous Elephants**
ISBN 978 0 7496 4634 9

**Freddie's Fears**
ISBN 978 0 7496 4382 9

**Squeaky Clean**
ISBN 978 0 7496 6805 1

**Craig's Crocodile**
ISBN 978 0 7496 6806 8

**Felicity Floss: Tooth Fairy**
ISBN 978 0 7496 6807 5

**Captain Cool**
ISBN 978 0 7496 6808 2

**Monster Cake**
ISBN 978 0 7496 6809 9

**The Super Trolley Ride**
ISBN 978 0 7496 6810 5

**The Royal Jumble Sale**
ISBN 978 0 7496 6811 2

**But, Mum!**
ISBN 978 0 7496 6812 9

**Dan's Gran's Goat**
ISBN 978 0 7496 6814 3

**Lighthouse Mouse**
ISBN 978 0 7496 6815 0

**Big Bad Bart**
ISBN 978 0 7496 6816 7

**Ron's Race**
ISBN 978 0 7496 6817 4

**Woolly the Bully**
ISBN 978 0 7496 7790 9

**Boris the Spider**
ISBN 978 0 7496 7791 6

**Miss Polly's Seaside Brolly**
ISBN 978 0 7496 7792 3

**Juggling Joe**
ISBN 978 0 7496 7795 4

**What a Frog!**
ISBN 978 0 7496 7794 7

**The Lonely Pirate**
ISBN 978 0 7496 7793 0

**I Wish!**
ISBN 978 0 7496 7940 8*
ISBN 978 0 7496 7952 1

**Raindrop Bill**
ISBN 978 0 7496 7941 5*
ISBN 978 0 7496 7953 8

**Sir Otto**
ISBN 978 0 7496 7942 2*
ISBN 978 0 7496 7954 5

**Queen Rosie**
ISBN 978 0 7496 7943 9*
ISBN 978 0 7496 7955 2

**Giraffe's Good Game**
ISBN 978 0 7496 7944 6*
ISBN 978 0 7496 7956 9

**Miss Lupin's Motorbike**
ISBN 978 0 7496 7945 3*
ISBN 978 0 7496 7957 6

**Alfie the Sea Dog**
ISBN 978 0 7496 7946 0*
ISBN 978 0 7496 7958 3

**Red Riding Hood Rap**
ISBN 978 0 7496 7947 7*
ISBN 978 0 7496 7959 0

**Pets on Parade**
ISBN 978 0 7496 7948 4*
ISBN 978 0 7496 7960 6

**Let's Dance**
ISBN 978 0 7496 7949 1*
ISBN 978 0 7496 7961 3

**Benny and the Monster**
ISBN 978 0 7496 7950 7*
ISBN 978 0 7496 7962 0

**Bathtime Rap**
ISBN 978 0 7496 7951 4*
ISBN 978 0 7496 7963 7

**Other Leapfrog titles also available:**

**Leapfrog Fairy Tales**

A selection of favourite fairy tales, simply retold.

**Leapfrog**

Fun, original stories by top authors and illustrators.

**For more details go to:**

www.franklinwatts.co.uk

* hardback

# Pets on Parade

First published in 2008 by
Franklin Watts
338 Euston Road
London
NW1 3BH

Franklin Watts Australia
Level 17/207 Kent Street
Sydney
NSW 2000

A CIP catalogue record for this book is available
from the British Library.

ISBN 978 0 7496 7948 4 (hbk)
ISBN 978 0 7496 7960 6 (pbk)

**Series Editor:** Jackie Hamley
**Editor:** Melanie Palmer
**Series Advisor:** Dr Barrie Wade
**Series Designer:** Peter Scoulding

Printed in China

Franklin Watts is a division of
Hachette Children's Books,
an Hachette Livre UK company.
www.hachettelivre.co.uk